## About the

**Kek-W** is a UK-based writer of comic-books, graphic novels, films, TV and fiction. He has written Horror, Fantasy, Science Fiction, Action-Adventure, War and Comedy-Satire.

His recent work includes JUDGE DREDD, ROGUE TROOPER and TYRANNY REX for *2000AD* / Rebellion Publishing, as well as the acclaimed DARK JUDGES: FALL OF DEADWORLD Dark Horror series featuring JUDGE DEATH, and the Historical Science Fantasy series THE ORDER.

He lives in the foul, flooded, sunlight-starved fenlands of the UK's West Country in a mobile stilt-hut from which he leads armed sorties against the region's despotic Hellbarons.

Contact: https://about.me/kekw

Also available:

THE RECONSTRUCTED MAN

THE NEW ABNORMAL

# OTHER TIMES

By

KEK-W

The Bicameral Press, Yeovil, Somerset

KEK-W asserts the moral right to be identified as the author of this work

Copyright (c) KEK-W 2024

This Edition Published by the Bicameral Press, March, 2024

Contains adult themes. Not for sale to minors.

Cover illustration 'My Heart' by Arthur Hughes. Out of Copyright and in the Public Domain.

All rights reserved. No part of this publication may be reproduced, stored in a retrieval system, or transmitted, in any form or by any means: electronic, mechanical, photocopying, recording or otherwise, without the prior permission of the publisher

This book is sold subject to the condition that it shall not, by way of trade or otherwise, be lent, re-sold, hired out or otherwise circulated without the author's prior consent in any form or binding other than that in which it is published and without a similar condition including this condition being imposed on the subsequent purchaser

**CONTENTS**

| | |
|---|---|
| **Mondo Baroque** | 7 |
| **Windward to Was-Not Island** | 63 |

"Real heroes are always impelled by circumstances; they never chose because, if they could, they would chose not to be heroes." - Umberto Eco, *Travels in Hyperreality*.

## MONDO BAROQUE

The Sinking City shivered and glowed like an opal in the pale, half-hearted light of dawn. Its buildings had a queer spectral quality – a sense of the temporary – as if the city was little more than a memory, vague and intangible, a dream that haunted its inhabitants every morning when they woke.

Stonework slowly took shape, sculpted by the light. As the sun rose over the East Lagoon the city grew increasingly solid, as if emerging from a dream and recasting itself in flagstones, plaster and stained glass. A bitter wind blew in from the salt marshes and twisted its way through a labyrinth of narrow streets and canals. The buildings seemed to stiffen at its touch, become more rigid, as if flaunting their new-found solidity.

Sound bled back into the world, carried by the wind. In the *Calle del Forno*, hooves clattered on cobble as a small procession of horsemen passed under the elaborate grey marble columns that supported the Bridge of Silver Shadows.

The sun rose over the lagoon and light splashed down from the mirrored mosaics on top of the Basilica Santa Lucia, patron saint of the blind. Amerigo Verde squinted and covered his eyes, glancing over his shoulder at the rag-tag company of religious dissidents and disgruntled republicans that rode behind him. Like Verde, they had been retained as bodyguards by Gian Guardi, a former senator who had survived the collapse of the old Republic. A price had been placed on Guardi's head when Rugerro IV, the self-proclaimed Pope of Wolves, had seized control of the Metropolitan Council earlier that spring. The pay was poor, but – being little more than an outlaw himself – Verde had no real cause for complaint.

Two streets from Guardi's fortified bolt-hole near the Moorish Quarter, they were ambushed.

Shuttered windows slammed open and a rain of crossbow bolts fell down upon them. His mount shied and a bolt narrowly missed Verde's neck, glancing instead off a leather epaulette. A second dart embedded itself in the horse's shoulder and the beast collapsed.

Verde quickly slid from the saddle, using the animal as a shield while he gathered his wits. More bolts thudded into its body. He watched as red-robed forms poured from nearby alleyways and doors, surrounding the horsemen, stabbing at them with pikes and hook-tipped poles. Their attackers wore wine-coloured hoods over grotesque bird-masks sculpted from copper and painted papier-mâché. Verde recognised their regalia as that of a Christian militia controlled by Monsignor Carpi, the so-called Red Cardinal.

Guardi's retinue was overrun in moments.

Guardi had taken a bolt in the breast-bone and a small, howling mob of bird-faced *bravos* were pulling him down from his horse. Verde felt little in the way of loyalty or concern; in fact, he had come to dislike this sour little man and his inane, bourgeois politics. Instead, he quickly calculated the odds of his own survival. They were not good.

The stricken horse lurched drunkenly away from him, rasping horribly. A militiaman lunged at Verde from his left. Remembering that they often wore breast-plates beneath their robes, Verde took the man, almost daintily, in the throat with his rapier. A second assailant he skewered through the wrist, the man sobbing like a child as he retreated.

Verde reached for his pistol, thinking he might run at a small group of them. If they were young and inexperienced, then he might break through their ranks and escape.

Instead, an ancient iron gate clanged open on a wall a few metres to his right and a figure stepped through. The newcomer was dressed in dark breeches and a doeskin vest, but moved with an obvious feminine grace. Her head was half-covered by a brown canvas cowl, but the skin of her face – what little he could see of it – seemed to be smooth and polished, as if sculpted from pewter. She raised a pistol – an elaborate pepper-box repeater of a design he was unfamiliar with –

and fired at their nearest attacker. The militiaman's mask exploded in a shower of copper and bone.

'Amerigo Verde!' She turned slightly as she shouted and he caught another glimpse of her face. It reminded him of an elaborate carnival mask embossed with ornate rococo swirls and motifs. *'Per di qua! Seguimi se desideri vivere!'* He nodded, her exotic silvered features making him feel strangely uncomfortable.

She fired the pistol again, sending a second assassin spinning sideways off into his comrades. A salvo of crossbow bolts converged upon her, ricocheting off her skin with a faint metallic ring.

Verde ran for the gate as she fired a third shot. She followed him through, snapping a padlock shut to thwart their pursuers.

They ran through a dimly lit alleyway, their boots crunching on rubble. Down some steps and along a water-logged gallery that ran parallel to a subterranean canal. The sluggish water glowed darkly, like oil, and was rimmed by a crust of vile brown foam.

Faint sunlight filtered down through grilles in the tunnel roof above. Small windows were embedded in the walls, some holding lanterns that cast flickering, distorted shadows. Pox-scabbed faces watched them hurry past.

He followed her with a mixture of fascination and growing unease. There was something unnatural about her movements. She possessed an athletic grace that bordered on the balletic, yet she seemed to swivel and twist in an overly stylised, almost sensual fashion, as if her limbs were connected by some armature other than the human skeleton.

The stream of filthy water eventually disappeared down a vertical, man-made weir. She led him to a concealed doorway on a ledge just below the cascade, then down a spiral stone staircase worn smooth by the years. At its bottom, a half-shattered oak door opened out onto the upper level of a vast, vaulted chamber which contained a number of half-ruined galleries and walkways. A helical spout of water corkscrewed from a fracture in the ceiling above them down into a small lake five stories or so below.

Down here, the architecture was angular and flat, bereft of the *barocco* flourishes favoured on the surface. There was no sense of pride or craftsmanship. On the walls were signs written in a language derived from Latin. Verde picked out words as they passed, phonemes that taunted him with their familiarity, but which were unreadable.

Some of the buildings had collapsed and folded in on themselves, compressed by the slowly sinking mass of the city above them. In places, the rubble had been crushed into discrete layers that slid downwards at forty-five degrees like ancient geological strata. Landslides seemed a common occurrence here: everywhere there were massive cracks and fissures, as if the whole weight of History was bearing down on them.

They picked their way downwards over cracked slabs of granite and beams of buckled iron. Someone had cemented alchemical glowstones onto the rubble, creating a pathway that illuminated the fractured landscape with a soft, white-blue light.

'Who are you?' asked Verde. 'Where are you taking me?'

'Massimo has a theory that these ruins are somehow *newer* than the ones above.' Her voice was rich and melodic as she gestured toward the strange flattened buildings, but it carried an odd sibilance, as if her breath came from tiny, mechanical bellows. He found himself strangely mesmerised, almost comforted by it. 'He believes that, at some point in the past, time temporarily inverted itself. That these ruins may have somehow originated from the *future*. Does that make sense?' She glanced back at him, her face bobbing like a distant moon in the sullen half-light.

'Perhaps,' he said, and shrugged. He was in no mood to speculate. 'I've heard of stranger things. Who is this Massimo?'

Her laugh was a harsh, breathy sound, like a breeze through a bell-tower. She continued walking ahead of him. 'You will meet him soon enough. He has a proposition he wants to put to you.'

'Obviously, I am in your debt, *signora,* but you clearly have me at an advantage.'

Another laugh. 'Your exploits are the talk of every tavern, Signor Verde. Soldier, poet, free-thinker… the Church accuses you of consorting with devils, while the Copernicans dismiss you as an anarchist mystic.'

This was nothing new to him. He answered without malice: 'Yes, it is true I am unpopular in certain quarters. I am what I am. And for that I make no apology.'

'I've heard odd stories concerning your wife. They say that she was... *lost* to you. The details are vague, but it's claimed that you squandered a fortune searching for her. There are a dozen different tales, some of them strange and fantastical.'

A cold void opened inside him, but he said nothing.

There was a hint of irony in her voice as she continued. 'Some say she died, others that she was abducted by *pesce pseuduomini* – fishmen from the Martian canals. They claimed you journeyed there to find her – that you explored the secret third moon of Earth in a balloon-ship built by the Cagliostro brothers. Or that you fought with ghostdogs on the mechanised island of Murano for a fragment of her soul.'

'Stories, that is all they are. And fanciful ones, at that,' commented Verde, coldly. '*Romanzi scientifici* – scientific romances printed purely for the purpose of entertainment and titillation. They can be bought in any marketplace for a quarter of a ducat. Some even say that I wrote them myself.'

'Ah, but even the most fanciful of tales sometimes have a grain of truth at their core.' She stopped suddenly and turned to look at him. He found himself wishing he could see her eyes. 'My name is Rhea del Bulgia, Signor Verde, and I am the closest thing you have to a friend right now.'

It was true, he supposed, but he nodded without much enthusiasm.

They had reached the edge of the black lake. Ripples pulsed across its surface, small waves created by the funnel of water that poured down from above. They trudged across a causeway made slippery by malignant mosses and algae. Vicious-looking albino fish glowered up at them from within the rock-pools.

'This place you are taking me... has it something to do with *her*? With my wife?' he asked.

She silenced him, placed a single leather-gloved finger to a softly silvered lip: '*Shhhh…*'

From across the lake came a series of awful, high-pitched howls. Rhea moved closer to him and spoke almost in a stage-whisper. 'Borgias! Degenerate, blood-bathing fiends – there is a colony of the creatures on the far side of the water. They must have caught your scent! Hurry, follow me! It's not far...' She jumped between cracked, cube-shaped slabs of granite rubble, nimbly, like a dancer from a *Commedia dell'arte* troupe, gesturing for him to follow.

Eerie, blood-curdling screeches and splashing sounds echoed across the lake behind them as they ran. There had been rumours of inbreeding and Satanic pacts, but Verde wondered how even a decadent aristocratic family such as the Borgias had degenerated so quickly into blood-addiction and complete savagery. The sounds that followed them across the broken, subterranean landscape were sub-human, almost feral.

Rhea leapt easily, with the grace of a ballerina, springing across any obstacles they encountered, while Verde's limbs stiffened and became sore, until they could no longer support his weight. He staggered, barely able to walk.

Seeing his obvious distress, she turned and took hold of him, almost dragging him along in her wake. Her arm felt rigid around his waist, metallic and unyielding. She was no woman, he realised, but some fabulous mechanism in the shape of one.

An automaton animated by intricate, internal cogs and gears, he imagined.

Behind them, the dreadful howls grew closer, so Rhea effortlessly hoisted him over her shoulder, carrying him as if he was a child.

Arcane sigils had been scratched and painted onto the rocks either side of a makeshift pathway. These took the form of malignant hexes and curses that were capable of inducing painful debility and eventual death. Unlike Verde, Rhea seemed oblivious to them. Pain blossomed in his belly like a dagger wound. He retched weakly.

He became increasingly feverish as the hex symbols weakened his body and distorted his mental faculties. In his delirium, he saw a vision of Maria, his missing wife. She stepped out from inside a shadow, her dark olive skin and tangle of black hair seeming so real that he feebly reached out in an attempt to touch her.

Maria tried to speak, but her smile cracked open as her mouth widened into a wound. Her flesh grew grey with corruption and rot, becoming dry and shrivelled until she took on the appearance of a mummified undead thing. She leaned closer until Verde could see every cut and lesion on her ruined face. Her bloodless lips opened to whisper something that he could not quite hear, yet knew was vitally important: a name, a place, some vital clue to his missing wife's whereabouts.

Rhea dropped him on the ground and he groaned with frustration as the vision abruptly vanished. She took a key from a chain that hung around her neck, using it to unlock an iron hatch set in the stone beneath them.

A circle of protective symbols surrounded the hatch. The Borgias – now massed on the other side of the circle – shuddered and moaned: pale, emaciated, stick-limbed things that writhed in the grey, uncertain light. The scent of Verde's blood had induced an animalistic delirium in them, but they seemed unwilling or unable to pass the occult boundary. Instead, they tested its strength, probed it for weaknesses or a gap, retreating as they brushed up against the barrier's invisible edges.

Driven insane by bloodlust, one of the creatures unexpectedly loped forward on impossibly thin, triple-jointed legs. Its gaunt, red-eyed face was chalk-dust white and topped by a ragged mass of scarecrow hair. Needle-sharp teeth lined a lipless, circular mouth. A long, black, worm-like tongue extended to lick at the air as it bounded forward towards them. Like the rest of the pack it was a female: the male bulls were huge and impossibly grotesque; they rarely left their blood-pools.

As it approached the circle it began to smoulder, then dramatically burst into flame, ignited by its proximity to the defensive hexes. But the Borgia continued to come at them, its limbs burning like old twigs, shrieking in indignation as it made a final, desperate lunge for the blood that would restore it. Rhea's pistol flared brightly in her hand, making a grisly ruin of the thing's burning head.

'Sorry, my dear,' said Rhea del Bulgia, mock-apologetically, as she stepped over its bony, smoking carcass and lowered Verde down through the hatch. 'But Signore Verde is already spoken for.'

***

They placed Verde on a comfortable chair in front of a roaring hearth in Massimo Cvarda's workshop. He was given brandy to drink and a homeopathic concoction that tasted faintly of vinegar and chalk, but which quickly restored his vigour.

Cvarda was a master alchemist whose workshop was a hive of activity. On the other side of the vast, stone-walled chamber, brass-plated automata shuffled through the steam and smoke, stoking furnaces and operating bellows. These hulking mechanical golems lacked Rhea's intelligence and grace, but were capable of efficiently performing a dozen different menial tasks.

Along one wall ran a network of glass tubes and pumps that drew an ochre-coloured gas through a series of water-cooled condensers and bubbling bell-jars. Arcs of blue-white lightning crackled and danced between copper coils, while Cvarda's clockwork men lumbered to and fro, transporting ingots of metal or drums filled with a pungent dark red oil.

As the brandy warmed his belly, Verde watched Rhea remove her gloves and slowly flex her slender fingers in a deliberate, almost contrived manner, as if she were fully aware she was being observed. Next, she slid the cowl down off her head, allowing him to see – as he had imagined – that her skull was smooth and hairless, and its shape was impossibly perfect, as were its proportions. Her skin reflected the fire that flickered in the wood-burner, giving her profile a warm, unearthly aura. She was a living statue cast from metal, sculpted by a master artisan.

He was surprised to discover just how much she fascinated him. Her features were fluid and expressive, not rigid and immutable as he had initially assumed.

He discretely watched subtle shifts in her expression, her face seemingly responding to changes in her innermost thoughts and emotions. Her skin was engraved with delicate lines and swirls that emphasised her high, aristocratic-looking cheeks. The sweep of her forehead suggested a deep intelligence, while the fullness of her silvered lips hinted at an unrestrained sensuality.

That she was beautiful was undeniable, but it was a form of beauty that Verde found difficult to name: she somehow combined the aesthetic virtues of both classical art and modern mechanical engineering with the natural God-given elegance of the female form. He was certain now that she was no mere automaton and that her remarkable metal body somehow housed a human soul.

He felt moved to touch her skin. Was it hard and unyielding – or smooth, delicate and warm to the touch? Or was that just wishful thinking on his part – an illusion created by the brandy and the workshop's sleepy light?

He wondered if she were alive in the conventional sense of the word. A hundred questions bubbled up in his mind, demanding answers. Did she eat? Breathe? Could she *feel?* Did she have a heart, a brain, a *soul?*

Cvarda, on the other hand, seemed a far more mundane character. He was a short, hairless man who was clearly in a state of poor health. One arm was withered, while the flesh on his face was uneven and ridged with scars, as if he had been a victim of some terrible plague or pox. One eye-socket and part of his jaw was patched with a soft leather covering.

He spoke with a coarse Neapolitan accent, punctuated by coughs. As he talked, he rubbed ointment onto the sores on his stricken skin. He claimed to have died, but had succumbed to some terrible disease in the Afterlife that had resulted in a peculiar death-in-reverse. This, he said, had returned him to life, but not to full health.

'Urbino's Syndrome,' said Verde, dryly. 'Named after a Florentine physician. He described patients of his that claimed to have fallen ill in Hell. His writings were banned by Benedict XII in a papal bull.'

'Aye. Dante also wrote of it too, but burned his lines for fear of being branded as a heretic. The Pope and his Christian warlords protect their power by ruling that resurrection is purely the province of Christ, not Man. If it became known that I was a returnee, then I would be arrested and put to the rack by Rugerro's Inquisitors – though their tortures would not kill me. Since my return, I can no longer die, and so would suffer indefinitely.' He coughed horribly, like an elderly consumptive. 'My lungs, my digestion... everything is failing. My bodily organs remained inactive while I lay cold in the tomb… my lungs filled with fluid, my flesh decayed. Soon, I will become immobile and riddled with tumours, but death, it appears, will be denied to me. I will remain conscious and alive while my body rots away around me.' He coughed again, wiped a watery smear of blood from his mouth. 'I use potions to slow the process, but my physical decline cannot be delayed indefinitely.'

'I see,' said Verde, but he felt oddly unmoved by Cvarda's plight. After his own loss, some essential inner part of himself had become submerged, lost to him. There were now gaps in his emotional palette, feelings he found hard to access. Although his instincts for self-preservation remained intact, he found he sometimes suffered from a form of acute anhedonia. A peculiar melancholy sometimes descended on him in which all ambition and passion abandoned him, and he would find himself drifting aimlessly from moment to moment, lacking in direction or focus. When the black dog held him firmly between its teeth, all hope seemed to evaporate. The world felt stripped of joy and meaning; life became hollow, vague and pointless.

And so, action had become a narcotic for him, an antidote of sorts. It provided a convenient distraction – a bridge across the strange, unnameable void that sometimes opened up within himself. Inactivity left him feeling empty.

Restless, he looked around for Rhea. His interest in her had started to extend beyond simple intellectual curiosity and was now, he realised, developing into a quiet infatuation. Whether this was a good or a bad thing, he could not say, but he welcomed the distraction. His quest for Maria now felt increasingly futile, and as he sat there surreptitiously studying Rhea he began to question its necessity. Perhaps it was time to finally acknowledge his loss and rebuild some sort of life for himself.

Cvarda rose awkwardly to his feet and beckoned for Verde to follow him across the workshop, past its hissing, groaning mechanical bellows and ratcheting, steam-driven pumps. On one wooden work-bench lay self-reflecting mirrors and ocular projectors that could peer into other planes of existence. Elsewhere, sat copper-plated listening horns lined with membranes cultured from living tissue that were attuned to sounds from the seven sun-circling worlds of Copernicus.

The body lay inside a steel sarcophagus, suspended inside a fine gossamer web of wires. It was a male metal counterpart to Rhea, smooth-skinned and perfectly proportioned in every way imaginable: an Apollo to her Diana.

As Verde studied its uncanny silver form something akin to jealousy rose up within him. That it was intended for Cvarda seemed obvious. He and Rhea would live forever, as demi-gods and mates.

Rhea, explained Cvarda, had also contracted Urbino's Syndrome in the Underworld. The pair had returned together and their fortunes were now inextricably entwined. Like Cvarda, her own health had rapidly deteriorated upon return.

'And so you constructed these machines to replace your own failing bodies,' Verde commented, dryly.

Cvarda coughed. The man was vain and proud, easily offended. Verde's words had irked him, as intended. '*Machines*? No, they are far more than that. They are synthetic bodies – perfect in every detail! I designed and built the device which spun them, like a loom, from metallic fibres. When I returned from the Other Side I brought back dark orphic knowledge – arcane techniques and formulae unknown to any other living man!'

Verde listened impassively to the man's boastful rant, but offered no praise, merely nodded. Wind a man up like a clockwork toy, starve him of complements and let him run off at the mouth – it was by far the quickest, most efficient way to obtain information, he had found. 'And you spun these bodies from silver?'

'No, no! It has the lustre of silver, but is known as *luna*. There is a second, secret Table of Elements known only to master alchemical adepts such as myself. Moon-metal is an analogue of silver but with properties that allow it to mimic human nerves. It is malleable and can transmit galvanic sensations, but it does not corrode.'

'Indeed. And you now intend to somehow transfer your mind or soul into it? As you did, I presume, with Rhea?'

'Of course,' said Cvarda, tartly. 'If I do not, then I am doomed. However, there is a complication…' He produced a small, milk-white, opal-like jewel from within his leather apron. 'Without this, the artificial body will not function. In layman's terms, it is the equivalent of the human heart. It provides the aetheric current that makes movement and tactile sensation possible. It links the mind to the artificial body by means of a thousand minute potential differences.'

'And this complication that you mentioned?' asked Verde. Rhea had joined them and now stood to one side of him, her arms folded, watching him. Her artificial eyes were a marvel: a pair of emeralds that floated in almond-shaped ovals of white.

'I have been swindled.' Cvarda held up the opal with a sour expression, his displeasure evident. 'This one was supposed to galvanise my new body, but it is flawed – woefully insufficient to the task. I bought a pair of these gems from Lacabro, an infamous local merchant who trades in rare and precious objects. Have you heard of him? The bastard is trying to blackmail me into giving *him* the secret knowledge I acquired in the Afterlife.'

'I see. And you require me to, what... *rebalance* this injustice?'

Cvarda's rant had left him temporarily breathless. He waited a moment, coughed into his fist, then continued. 'Delicately put. He expects me to dispatch Rhea – who he alone possesses the means to destroy. He will not be anticipating a human agent such as yourself. Naturally, I will reward you handsomely for your efforts.'

'Naturally.' Verde fell silent, pretending to ponder the offer. Cvarda's story contained a number of implausible elements. The alchemist almost certainly intended to double-cross him at some point in the proceedings.

But then a sudden stray thought consumed him: what if he, Amerigo Verde, were somehow able to take both the metal body *and* Rhea as his own? To be placed inside a sheath of silver skin could be no worse than being trapped in the flimsy, hollow shell he currently occupied. He would be indestructible, *immortal...* the two of them could travel together, explore the far ends of the universe. The idea was ridiculous, he knew – little more than a childish fantasy – yet it held an undeniable allure.

However, there were too many unknown variables. If he killed Cvarda, for example, then how would he take possession of the body? And Rhea's own loyalties undoubtedly lay with the alchemist. How could he convince her to join him?

'I have something that might interest you,' said Cvarda. 'Consider it a retainer for your services.'

He shuffled off, coughing, toward a set of shelves containing bottles labelled in Latin and filled with coloured tinctures. He returned holding a necklace. 'I believe this once belonged to your wife,' he said.

Verde snatched it from him. He studied it intently, looking for signs of fraud.

'Where did you get this?' he snapped. He grabbed Cvarda roughly by the shoulders. 'Tell me or I'll kill you.'

To his left, he saw Rhea slowly remove her pistol from its holster. Her expression was blank, without pity.

Verde's senses had become painfully sharp. He could smell Cvarda's sour breath and the pungent liniments on his dying skin. The alchemist matched Verde's fierce gaze with his remaining good eye. 'Perform this one task for me and I will gladly tell you.'

***

The journey back to the surface passed without incident, as Cvarda had supplied Verde with the appropriate counter-charms. Rhea accompanied him, but a strange atmosphere had settled over the pair. The necklace had unnerved him. Verde asked a few vague questions about Lacabro, but mostly he brooded, searching deep within himself for the source of his dissatisfaction.

Early evening found them walking briskly down the *Via Rosso* towards The Floating Square. Rhea hid her features deep within her cowl and kept to the shadows, avoiding the gaze of other pedestrians. In the gutters sat brown-robed beggars with empty eye-sockets, zealots from some obscure monastic sect who had blinded themselves with lime and vinegar.

As the street lamps were lit, Verde found his spirits slowly lifting. As night fell, the Sinking City came back to life, its brightly decorated *gallerias* and covered walkways rousing him from what now felt like an oppressive dream.

In the narrow arcades of the Rialto, they passed stalls that sold glassware and intricate, off-white Burano lace. Tables covered in grotesque death-masks, cameos and *momento mori*; hawkers with trunks full of extravagant *maschera*, paste jewellery and fancy-dress costumes from the previous year's carnival season. Mynah birds watched them suspiciously from painted cane cages. There were bookcases stuffed with musty, flat-spined books in wooden bindings that dated back to the Romanesque Era. Folios and scrolls whose doe vellum pages were filled with delicate, mould-speckled illustrations of mythical beasts and impossible mechanical inventions. Lurid surgical text-books sketched by Salaì, a former pupil of da Vinci, that purported to show the internal organs and workings of a dissected fallen angel.

As they emerged at the edge of the square, opposite the bakeries and *pasticceria*, a steam calliope played a lively tune with a cascading melody-line – a *saltarello* – a folk-dance that was still popular in the Montefeltro Region. Beneath its garish red and gold-painted whistles a mechanical monkey frolicked with a clockwork harlequin. In the thoroughfare opposite, a group of shop-girls drank wine and giggled at the performing automata, raising the hems of their skirts to dance a merry jig.

Rhea led him past the women, down a flight of steps and across the Bridge of Lies with its cracked plaster cherubs and intricate red enamel devils. Wood creaked beneath his feet and water slapped lazily against the ancient stone walls of the canal below. In the distance Verde heard the roar of the crowd in the Taurean Arena. Now they followed a narrow, run-down waterway that the locals called the Tears of Venus. Drunken singing came from a balcony somewhere high above them. A dead dog floated in the dark, stagnant water.

'Down here,' said Rhea, indicting a warehouse with its own small wooden jetty. Dull, tired-looking light leaked out from within.

Her voice, which had so enchanted him a few hours earlier, now irritated, even angered him. Away from the bright lights and the busy hubbub Verde's mood had darkened once again. What was it about Rhea that had provoked this sense of unease in him? He tried to understand his feelings.

Was it just childish jealousy, he wondered, or some innate disquiet at her supernatural origins? Or had his subconscious, perhaps, recognised some terrible, unpalatable truth about her?

An odd idea began to form in his head and he chuckled under his breath at his own idiocy. But before he could act on the thought, Fate intervened and he found himself drawing his sword.

Exactly what had alerted him to the attack, he could not say. Perhaps he had heard some soft, almost subliminal sound or had caught sight of a vague movement in the corner of his eye? He had been ambushed already once that day and had promised himself that there would be no repetition.

Their assailants slid out from the shadows, resembling characters from some some horrific satirical farce that might have been staged in the Teatro dell'Assurdo e del Grottesco. They were militiamen, he initially assumed, dressed in rough canvas tunics and a raggle-taggle assortment of helmets and caps. One had a pantomime skull painted on his face, but Verde quickly realised that this pale, shrivelled visage was neither a mask nor greasepaint.

He took the creature through the shoulder above its leather breast-plate. Whatever it was, it squealed like a wild pig as it staggered away from him. He followed through, slashing at its face, his blade finding solid yellow bone, not flesh.

A second attacker was already upon him. Verde took a glancing blow to the side of the head with a weighted pole or staff. Somehow he managed to avoid the backswing, though he felt the air move in front of him, a whisker away from his face as he stumbled backwards, off-balance. He grabbed at the pistol in his belt with his left hand, pulled it out and shot the pasty-faced devil at close quarters.

The thing lurched away from him, dropped its staff, but did not fall. Verde discarded his pistol and stabbed at its side with his rapier. He pushed hard upon its hilt, hoping to find a vulnerable organ or weak spot within its guts. He twisted off to one side past it, grunting with effort and hearing a satisfyingly wet sound as his sword slid free. His inhuman opponent made a gurgling sound as fluids filled its mouth, then stumbled sideways off into the shadow.

'Rhea!' cried Verde, but there was no answer.

Another attacker lurched forward into the light, leering at him with its thin, lipless mouth. Verde stabbed at it with his sword, but was struck down from behind.

His vision lit up, his eyes filling with bright winter stars and streamers of multi-coloured light – like a firework display at the *Festa del Redentore* – then his eye-sight darkened and his skull emptied itself of all thoughts. Verde's legs grew weak and soft beneath him, no longer able to bear his weight, and he collapsed.

He lay on his side, numb and unable to move, his head orbiting itself like a clockwork orrery. He felt inexplicably cold. Fragments of gravel pressed against his cheek like tiny knives; the sheath of his dagger dug into his hip. He smelled dog piss in the weeds beside his face, heard water in the nearby canal chuckling at his stupidity and misfortune.

The world spun dizzily as someone lifted him off the ground. His senses temporarily left him again until he was casually dropped onto a wooden floor a few minutes later. He opened his eyes, but they failed to register a coherent image. Guttural voices spoke in a harsh, unintelligible language. He heard Rhea's voice, caught a blurred glimpse of her boots as they passed briefly through his line of sight.

'I have kept my side of the bargain and delivered Verde to you,' she said to someone he could not see. 'Now you must honour yours. Is the machine ready? Massimo is growing impatient for the soulstone to be charged.'

Verde heard a sound that resembled an enormous buzzing insect. *Was it a voice? If not, then... what?* He tried to make sense of it, but his thoughts were vague and disconnected.

Now he was being dragged boot-first across floorboards. He glimpsed shelves packed with glass jars of phosphoros, cinnabar and arsenic. Purple permanganate crystals and powdered sulfur glistened in the flickering lamp-light. There were cases full of bulky, leather-bound books; statues depicting satyrs and animal-headed entities from some lost pantheon.

His head throbbed as he returned to full consciousness. They had stripped him of his dagger and his other weapons, but he was relieved to find they had missed the small stiletto he kept strapped to his left forearm. The blade had been honed to needle-thin sharpness and was designed to slide inside a man's heart and burst it, though he quickly realised how ineffectual this would be against Rhea's metal skin.

He focused instead on his surroundings and decided that he was inside Lacabro's warehouse. Nearby, Rhea was talking. *But to who? The mysterious Lacabro, perhaps?* There was anger and bitterness in her voice. 'I want Verde fully awake when your machine sucks the fluid from his brain. I want it to *hurt*. I want to look into his eyes as he dies.'

More buzzing sounds, then a low, masculine voice, coarse and unearthly: 'After we have drained him, one of my brood will wear his corpse, as we agreed. My young are eager to wear warm human meat. Verde's aura is particularly virile and succulent, as you said it would be.'

'Indeed,' she replied, 'If you are looking for a human puppet to help spark an insurrection against the Cardinals, then Verde is the perfect choice. He has become something of a folk-hero amongst the idiotic peasant classes. His exploits have assumed a life of their own – though he seems oblivious to his own growing fame. If one of your offspring were to assume his identity you could turn this to your advantage.'

The way she spoke seemed familiar, confirming his earlier suspicions. Her words triggered a series of splintered reminiscences. In his mind's eye he saw a cortège of funeral barges passing through the faded splendour of La Canal Grande. Sprays of black lilies. Mahogany coffins containing the bodies of his sister, brother and uncle. They slept now in the vast walled necropolis that lay on the Sinking City's eastern peninsula, past the Mortician's Quarter.

A sudden wave of emotion washed over him, but he refused to allow himself to succumb to confusion and despair. Instead, he let his anger galvanise him, allowed it to banish the pain and weariness. His mind raced, calculated odds, formulated strategies. He tried to gauge how many were present in the room and their relative positions.

Rhea desired him alive – if only to goad and torture him – so her allies might momentarily hesitate before bringing lethal force to bear. This might buy him a few additional seconds. Every moment would be precious; he could not afford to waste a single movement. He needed to get in amongst them quickly and wreak havoc. The odds were near-impossible, he knew, but he would die honouring his family.

The queer-sounding, insect-like voice spoke again. 'Once we assume human-form, we can play the city's ruling factions off against each other. Sow the seeds of rebellion and discontent amongst the common folk.'

'Yes, a civil war would leave all parties weakened, except for yourselves,' agreed Rhea. 'Charge the soulstone for me, and Massimo will aid your plans for conquest. He can design weapons for you: unstoppable clockwork war-machines, steam-driven dreadnoughts.'

Seeing Verde's eyes flicker and move, she kicked viciously at his ribs. A pair of repulsive skull-faced ghouls hoisted him to his feet. In the light, he could now see they were Deaths Head mercenaries – undead soldiers from Transcarpathia who sold their swords to the highest bidder. Their uniforms were worn and dirty and smelled of the grave. One of them leered at him, its sallow, waxy skin crinkling like the pages of an old book. Verde feigned weakness, pretending to stagger as they pushed him towards her.

Rhea grabbed at his jerkin with a silver fist, pulling him closer. 'Before you die, I want you to know who I am.'

'I believe I have already guessed,' he said. 'You call yourself Rhea, but you are my dear, departed wife, Maria.' His mouth twisted into a sour mask of contempt, his words dripping with ironic venom.

'Who you yourself killed,' she said, coldly.

'You betrayed us to our enemies. They destroyed my family – killed my closest friends. And for that I despise you.'

'You are weak and sentimental, Amerigo. A fool who is content to drift on the tide of history.'

'Yes, you're right: I *am* a fool – a fool to have loved you like I did,' he said, sadly. 'I know that now. A seer I consulted on the Avenue of the Lost warned me that you had returned from the grave. I devoted all my energies to hunting you down. I won't rest until you are returned to Hell.' He allowed his left arm to hang limply at his side – pretended to rub it, as if it was injured – while he positioned his thumb near the clasp that held his stiletto.

'Well, you've found me now,' she sneered, the soft melodic resonance in her voice replaced by a harsh metallic ring. 'But this encounter will not end as you hoped, husband dear. I intend to avenge my own murder. Your life-force will be drained and used to power Massimo's new metal body, while your own mindless body will be used as a vehicle by our allies from the Crimson Abyss. A delicious irony, don't you think?' With her other hand Rhea held up the soulstone and taunted him with it. She glanced towards Lacabro, a stocky, middle-aged patrician, who nodded imperceptibly.

'Fetch the machine,' ordered Lacabro. His voice sounded odd, as if he had not properly mastered the use of his own throat.

A trio of undead mercenaries dragged forth an arcane contraption made from brass and lacquered wood. A set of drills and steel needles were connected to the box by thin, flexible tubes made from some dark, vulcanised material. It had levers and a steam-driven pump, gauges to measure galvanic responses and a recess into which the soulstone could be slotted.

While they tended to the device, Verde made his move.

He popped the clasp, dropping the stiletto down his sleeve and into the palm of his hand. He lunged forward, stabbing at Rhea's eyes with it. Her eyes, he had reasoned, were the only part of her body not made from metal. Their artificial irises and lenses were vulnerable to an attack. She howled in outrage, releasing him as she tried in vain to protect her sight.

Verde snatched the soulstone and pocketed it. He darted behind her, grabbing her pistol from its holster. Using her as a shield, he fired at the nearest mercenary. The ghoul crumpled as the shot shattered its breast bone.

Lacabro's mercenaries were slow to respond. Verde fired at another of them, and another after that, sewing confusion and uproar amongst his enemies.

Lacabro disappeared from view, hiding himself behind a stone buttress. A blunderbuss roared, but Rhea's body protected him from most of the shrapnel. Some shot grazed his side, but he ignored the pain.

Rhea hissed with indignation as she swatted at him blindly with her fists. But he twisted away, out of reach, and shot another of the foul, unliving soldiers. The thing staggered and flailed its arms, issuing a high-pitched keening sound. Even though it was already dead, he had *damaged* it in some obscure way.

The repeater pistol was now either empty or had jammed, so Verde discarded it. He ran for the shelves loaded with chemical jars, recognising the alchemical symbol for phosphoros and its uncanny green-white glow. He hurled one of the glass bottles at Rhea. It shattered on her chest, its contents igniting with a sudden white-hot flare. Her clothes caught fire. The chemical stuck to her like burning glue.

He threw more of the jars, one after another, each exploding as they struck her metal body, which now burned with a lurid white fire that gave off an acrid stink.

In desperation Rhea tried to scrape the hot, burning phosphoros from her moon-metal skin, but it stuck to her hands now too and could not be removed. The chemical burned fiercely, reacting with her pseudo-silver flesh, which began to soften and melt. She screamed, but it was an awful, inhuman, *mechanical* sound.

The phosphoros spat and hissed, splattering onto the floorboards and a ghoul's uniform. The Deaths Head soldiers seemed wary of the fire, so Verde threw a jar in amongst them, then snatched a lantern down from its fitting and flung this toward them too. As the burning oil ignited the floorboards, the creatures shrunk away from it, growling and moaning amongst themselves like nervous animals.

Heartened by this turn of events, he pulled at the shelving until the entire wooden cabinet came away from the wall and crashed down on them in a riot of smashing glass. As well as phosphoros, there were also jars containing magnesia, sodium and other volatile compounds that erupted violently, like Chinese fireworks, spitting coloured flame when exposed to the air. There was now a burning barricade between himself and the Transcarpathians. The ghouls made fearful hissing sounds as they retreated from the fire and disappeared from view down a back flight of stairs.

Rhea's body warped grotesquely, the moon-metal dripping from her form like hot, melting tallow. Her limbs lengthened and bent out of shape. She howled in anguish, crying out for help as her arms and legs ceased to obey her. Verde watched with grim indifference as her still-burning body fused into a single twisted mass of blackened silver.

Verde heard the odd buzzing sound again and turned as Lacabro came at him, swinging a metal axe with both hands. He hurled himself sideways, but the blade took an agonising slice from the flesh in his shoulder. Lacabro swung at him again, but Verde threw himself backwards onto the floor, the axe missing his head by the length of a finger.

His back to the bonfire, Verde looked around for a weapon. His hand came upon a length of burning wood, which he threw at the merchant's face. The axe-head thudded into the floorboards next to him as he rolled away and tried to regain his footing.

Lacabro stood facing him, strangely inert. The merchant's mouth opened, widening further than any human mouth was meant to. There was a dull crack as Lacabro's jaw dislocated itself. A series of small, fleshy tendrils now extruded themselves from his maw. The venomous-looking mouth-parts began to vibrate rapidly in the air, making an eerie, insect-like drone. Lacabro's eyes rolled back in their sockets and were replaced by an amber-coloured film. His fingers quivered like the antennae of an excited moth, gelatinous drool leaked from his over-stretched lips.

Verde shuddered. Lacabro was obviously possessed – or rather, *inhabited* – by some vile insect thing. Was this the terrible fate that Maria had intended for him – to suck all thought from his skull and invite some loathsome, otherworldly parasite to wear his skin?

The monster's call was answered by a series of high-pitched buzzing sounds. On a nearby wall, attached to the stonework by a dark, resinous substance that resembled malignant honey, was a peculiar structure that resembled a wild wasps' nest. Each waxy, polygonal cell held a wriggling mass of tiny tentacles that vibrated like living tuning-forks and emitted a shrill insectoid sound. The creatures were partially hidden within their protective cells, but the parts that were exposed resembled some ghastly amalgam of anemone and cuttlefish. Verde had no doubt that this honeycomb structure was some form of alien hatchery or nursery.

As the fire spread across the floorboards towards them, the sound made by these creatures grew in intensity. Smoke swirled upwards, forming a thick, dark fug below the ceiling. Soon the air would be unbreathable.

'Your children!' cried Verde, desperately trying to reason with Lacabro. His shirt was now soaked with blood from the shoulder wound and he could feel his strength ebbing away from him. 'If you act now, you can still save them!'

But the creature was beyond logic or reason. Propelled by some unknowable alien rage, it launched itself at Verde. The pair of them rolled and slid backwards across the floorboards, grappling until they collided with the machine designed to charge the soulstone.

Verde snatched up one of its needle-like attachments and thrust it into the obscene, pulpy mass of tentacles that writhed inside Lacabro's mouth. Lacabro shuddered with pain as if he had been stabbed by a dagger.

A pale, glue-like substance leaked from the damaged tendrils and the thing loosened its grip on Verde slightly. Verde thrust the metal needle deeper into Lacabro's mouth until it struck his jawbone. Lacabro choked, tried to cry out, let out a sound somewhere between a gurgle and a rasp.

Rancid liquid oozed from Lacabro's ruined mouth, flecked with blood and grue. It dripped on Verde's hands as he pushed the merchant's head away from him and engaged the pump. The small engine hissed and spluttered into life, drawing a mixture of blood and semi-liquefied, piss-coloured adipose tissue up through the pipe.

Lacabro squirmed and shook as Verde held him by the throat and stabbed at him with a whirring drill-bit. The machine's piercing whine seemed to harmonise with the buzzing and burring sounds made by Lacabro's offspring. Verde crawled out from under the shuddering thing and finished it off with the axe.

He felt light-headed and sick now, coughing as acrid smoke filled his lungs. His injured shoulder throbbed. Maria's smouldering, half-melted body was too hot to touch, so he used a staff abandoned by one of the retreating mercenaries to push and lever it towards a nearby window. Oddly, she weighed little more than a normal woman, as if the metal that formed her body had some spectral density that made it unnaturally light.

Her alchemechanical innards had become molten – her clockwork organs temporarily liquefying and bursting out from within, as if she had been eviscerated. These had now cooled and hardened outside her, forming bulbous blossoms and dark, tumour-like growths on her fire-blackened skin which resembled the bracket fungi that erupted from tree trunks in the Autumn damp.

Maria's sole remaining eye peered out at him through a thin veil of twisted metal tissue. The artificial iris dilated slightly as it watched him with evil intent, confirming what he suspected: that she was still alive, but trapped inside the fused mass of Fools Silver.

Verde pushed and kicked at her immobile body, until it crashed through the window in a shower of shattered glass, falling into the canal below. Air rushed in to feed the fire, which seemed to literally explode behind him, and he was pushed out through the window-frame and down into the water below.

Shivering with cold and exertion, Verde pulled himself from the canal, crawling on all fours into the weeds where he vomited. Flames from the warehouse windows were reflected in the brackish water below. Verde watched light dance across the surface of the water like facets of an exotic fire-gem as he coughed up water and smoke.

Clutching at his wounded shoulder, Verde staggered up a flight of worn stone steps towards the thoroughfare above. There was a unlicensed physician he knew who had a backroom surgery in a courtyard beneath the Bridge of Grey Circles. He was a grizzled old Gaul with sad eyes and hair the colour of dirty sand – a Republican sympathiser who bathed Verde's wound with carbolic and packed it with medicinal herbs to draw out the poisons.

The fever hit him on the second day and Verde was tormented by visions of Maria's ghostly white face tangled in weeds as she drifted in the bottle-green murk at the bottom of the canal. When his strength had returned, he hired some Romany *bravos* to help him drag the canal until they finally pulled her ruined metal body from the water.

Although he detected no movement in her remaining eye, he had no doubt that her consciousness still resided somewhere within the soulstone. He wondered what would happen if her physical form were destroyed? Would her soul return to Hell or would she merely cease to exist?

He speculated on a number of possible metaphysical outcomes before finally ordering her remains to be consigned to the furnace.

\*\*\*

Armed with the appropriate protective charms, Verde returned to Cvarda's subsurface lair and hammered on the hatch, demanding entrance. 'Let me in! I have the soulstone,' he yelled. 'It has been charged with a human life-force!'

Eventually, the alchemist answered, as he knew he would. 'Where is Rhea?' he shouted from within. 'What have you done with her?'

'She is dead!' said Verde, blandly. 'The pair of you schemed to kill me. She has paid the price for your double-dealings. I disposed of her and negotiated my own alliance with Lacabro. I have the soulstone with me and would trade it with you for gold! This stand-off profits no one, Cvarda. I propose that we put our differences behind us. What do you say?'

Cvarda considered this for a few moments, then answered: 'Very well! I will barter with you. As you say, there is no reason for us to be enemies…'

A minute or two later, the hatch opened and one of Cvarda's clockwork monstrosities emerged. It had a repeating-pistol mechanism in place of a hand and climbed forth in search of Verde, its electrochemical eyes sparking in the gloom.

Verde had carefully removed each of the protective hexes and charms that surrounded the hatch, so that a brood of shrieking, blood-starved borgias swarmed over the hapless automaton and into Cvarda's workshop below. As Verde climbed back up towards the surface, the alchemist's screams echoed out across the lake like the cry of some awful demonic bird.

*\*\*\**

Later that summer, Verde had almost exhausted his funds. Without Cvarda's arcane expertise the spare soulstone was almost worthless – little more than a curio – so he had sold it to a dealer in trinkets and costume jewellery. Now he took up residence in a private booth at the back of a smoky bistro on the *Calle del Verno,* where he sat with a stylus and a pile of vellum. It was his intention to write, under a pseudonym, a stylised fictional account – a *romanzo fantasy* or, rather, a *ucronia* – of his adventures with the mechanical woman, Rhea, in the fabulous underground world of Città Sommersa.

As he assembled his thoughts into some sort of narrative order he imagined Cvarda's mindless clockwork men, still stumbling endlessly through the ruins of the workshop, carrying out the same repetitive menial tasks again and again.

*How strangely similar to human beings they are,* he thought as he sipped at a cup of sour red wine. *Even with the benefit of hindsight and free will, we seem doomed to forever make the same mistakes. We sleepwalk through our lives, eating and drinking and falling in love with the same people, over and over again.*

Then he recalled how, when Maria's body had been reduced to a dull, silver-tinged slag by the furnace, he had surprised himself by having a small moon-silver locket fashioned from part of her white-hot remains. He wore it for a while on the necklace-chain he had taken from Cvarda, until finally, on a whim, he had gifted it to a prostitute he had become fond of – a woman whose dark grey-blue eyes flashed and sparkled like winter sunshine on the deep, wind-stirred waters of the East Lagoon.

And, with that image still fresh in his mind, he smiled to himself, drank another draught of the bitter wine, took up his pen and began to write.

# WINDWARD TO WAS-NOT ISLAND

My wife had finally wearied of my idle ways and had thrown me out a few days earlier, so I was somewhat down and a little at odds with myself at the time. I had toyed with the idea of taking up carpentry as a profession, seeing as I was handy with tools and such, but I still had salt in my blood and the idea of settling down on dry land had little appeal for someone with itchy bones such as myself.

I was kicking around at a loose end, looking for a berth, when I bumped into Briggsy – William Briggs – with whom I had served on the *Harkaway* under Old Man Michaels. Age had not improved him much and he still had that wild, faraway look in his eyes, but a few ales and an hour or two in his company did much to improve my humour. There is much to be said for the way that a pewter tankard catches the sleepy, amber light of an open fire.

'Listen, Sean,' he said, tapping out his pipe on the edge of the table, 'I've got something that might interest you…' He leaned forward and lowered his voice, so I could barely hear him over the busy taproom hubbub. 'It's easy money – or so I'm lead to believe. But you mustn't breathe a word of this to another soul.'

I scratched at my beard and nodded. 'You have my word.'

He grinned at me, showing off the gap where he had lost a tooth in a brawl in Lisbon. 'Good. Look, I'd been hoping to run into you. I'm shipping out tomorrow on the *Woolsey* and they need another deck-hand. I could put in a word for you. What d'you say?' He looked round warily. 'The pay is outrageous,' he whispered. 'Ten Sovereigns for two or three week's work…'

'Ye Gods.' I exhaled noisily into my pot. 'Then it'll be dirty work, for certain.' I weighed up the odds. I'd spent 100 days in Bodmin Gaol at His Majesty's Pleasure some years back and had no desire to return to a cess-pit such as that, yet the money would set me back on my feet. 'Two weeks, you say. Then, it's not a quick rum run to the continent and back. Billy, you know I've no stomach for killing and such.'

He shook his head. 'The skipper seems a decent enough sort. A Swede or a Norwegian – I forget which – name of Liestøl. And the crew aren't a bad lot either, what I've seen of them. One or two old hands you might recognise.' He lowered his voice until it was little more than a snake-like hiss. 'The money's to buy our silence, Sean, me boy. It's hush money. Our destination's a secret, but we'll not be crossing swords with any Customs men.'

I wasn't convinced, but Briggsy had always had a certain boyish charm about him. He smiled and winked playfully, raising his pot to toast a nearby serving lass. She beamed back at him, then, a moment later, looked coyly back over her shoulder to see if he was eyeing her behind. But when I tried to catch the girl's attention in a similar fashion, she turned away, coldly, and I felt the years close in on me and there was a sudden gnawing sadness within me that I didn't want to put a name to. I finished my ale and thought it over while Briggsy restocked his pipe. I wasn't getting any younger. Perhaps my running days were coming to an end, after all. The money might, I decided, put me back in good stead with my wife.

But a sense of unease had settled on me now like a heavy blanket and I hoped that God Almighty could forgive me for any dirty deeds I might have to perform in the employ of our mysterious paymaster.

\*\*\*

Despite my misapprehension, I felt strangely alive when I met with Billy Briggs the following morning. The breeze from the harbour felt as sharp as my senses and carried a pungent aroma of fish, salt and freshly painted pitch. Ropes creaked and water slapped against stone as we weaved our way through the quayside bustle, past the stalls and vendors who had set up outside the Customs House.

I had brought a bag with me from my lodgings packed with a few paltry belongings: some clean duck trousers, a heavy cloth jacket and cap; a razor, comb and a knot of soap. Tucked away beneath the linen were a French naval pistol and a pouch of shot I had won from a drunken matelot in Marseilles. Its weight gave me a much-needed feeling of comfort.

The *Woolsey* was a small merchant schooner in need of a little repair, but it was still afloat and that was good enough for me. Briggsy had put in a word, as he said he would, and led me over to Myers, the mate, a sallow-faced man with small, sunken, bead-like eyes who looked me over, sniffing at my breath and checking my arms for signs of pox. He asked a few terse questions and, seeming satisfied with the answers, grunted and aimed a thumb towards the gangplank.

We spent the morning loading provisions: barrels of salted beef; vinegar, beans and cheese.

Within a few minutes I had settled into the familiar, almost tender rhythm of work and soon it felt as if I had been born with a knotted rope in my hand. As we followed the tide out of Dartsmouth, a brisk sou'westerly began to fill our sails and my recent misgivings were soon forgotten. The wind made my skin tingle. My thoughts began to race excitedly in a manner I had not felt for many weeks. The brightly-painted dockside cottages quickly drifted away from us and the rolling hills of Devon were soon lost in a haze of mist and spray.

*Why is it*, I wondered, *that the familiar only becomes precious to us when we leave it?*

\*\*\*

Liestøl, the captain, was a queer-looking duck with thin grey hair and deathly pale skin that seemed as if it had been stretched over his skull. He had the look of a man who had had one too many close encounters with the Reaper. Captain in name only, he left the seamanship to Myers and Mr. Nichols the bosun, preferring instead to remain in his cabin, emerging only occasionally to chart our course with an arcane-looking brass mechanism the likes of which I had never seen before.

Three days out, he addressed the crew in heavily-accented English beneath an overcast, colourless sky, his eyes burning with a fierce inner light. We would be entering strange waters, he warned us, uncharted regions where the laws of God and Nature were routinely ignored. In the days to come, we would witness a great many wonders, sights that would turn most men's heads. He cautioned us to remain calm, to keep our minds open and our heads clear. The work would be hard, but the rewards even greater. He signalled to Myers, who handed out a sovereign to each crew-member.

Beside me, Frenchie DuBois crossed himself and scowled under his breath in broken English to Briggsy and myself: 'The man's a lunatic, *mes amis*. But who am I to argue where money is concerned?'

\*\*\*

As we left the Channel and headed out into the Atlantic, Liestøl assembled a strange-looking metal contraption on the main-deck. It burned a dark, peat-like fuel and belched rank, oily smoke from a tangle of copper pipes. Myers set a fire-watch rota to keep the infernal machine stoked, as per the captain's whim. And so it spewed forth acrid fumes and issued a constant high-pitched whining sound which set the crew's teeth on edge. At night, eerie orange and plum coloured lights flickered inside the tiny windows on the brass dome that capped its body.

  Our speed soon doubled, then trebled, and much of our time was spent repairing rips in the sails, which ballooned obscenely and often tore, as if filled by a fierce, imaginary wind. The water around the *Woolsey* grew increasingly dark, streaked with morbid, bruise-coloured purples, while the clouds above us seemed to boil, though the storms they threatened never quite materialised.

Frenchie had been busy fishing. He had it in his mind to add some variety to the galley's drab, colourless fare, but I had never seen anything as queer or vile as the thing that he hauled out of the water on the ninth day. This fish (if fish it was) was the size of a dog, with a squat, barrel-like body that flapped and rolled around on the deck, snarling like an enraged fox-terrier, the baited hook still piercing its snout lips. We beat upon it, repeatedly, with oars until it ceased its awful, shrill yelping.

When Frenchie gutted the creature, he found it had *lungs*, not gills. I shudder to remember, but those that partook of its flesh swore that it was succulent and tasted like lamb, but was somewhat bitter. That evening, I cleaned my pistol and loaded it as a precaution, but against what I knew not.

***

A strange mood settled on the crew. It felt as if we were sailing into a dream, albeit an old, familiar one, something half-remembered from childhood, whose ending cannot quite be recalled, but was undoubtedly tragic. Frenchie says there's a name for this strange, half-awake feeling: "Déjà vu."

As I laid in my canvas hammock at night listening to the timbers creak and the water surging and churning in the darkness beneath us, it seemed almost as if the boat was sailing itself, guided by Liestøl's uncanny mechanism, and we were its passengers – wayfarers whose destination had been chosen by forces beyond their comprehension.

Divorced from female companionship, Briggsy's usual easy charm had soured. He became quiet and sullen, as if he could no longer tolerate his own company. Myers, wise old egg that he was, kept us all busy repairing the rigging and pumping the bilges, so that our fear and discontent never fully surfaced. There is much to be said, I believe, for the virtues of hard, honest labour.

***

One night, in the small hours of midwatch, I spied a faint light coming from Liestøl's cabin. Curiosity got the better of me and I cautiously approached from the larboard side to take a peek, whereupon I heard his muffled voice come from within.

I strained to hear his words against the slap of the waves before realizing that he was addressing someone in his native tongue: '*Nederdrektige beist! Allerede har du tatt fra meg min familie, og alle jeg holder kjær, er ikke det nok? Hvorfor fortsetter du å plage meg slik? Har jeg ikke sverget å bringe deg tilbake til dit du kom fra...?*'

Peering through the small, smeary, lead-framed panes, I could make out Liestøl's warped silhouette lit by what I thought was a flickering lantern... until the light suddenly began to move in an odd fashion, seemingly zigzagging through the air, casting sinister shadows that twisted and lengthened in a grotesque, unnatural manner. Then I heard a sound come from within the cabin that made my blood run cold.

It was a voice, but one that resembled the vile squawk of a Punchinello puppet. I knew instantly that no human mouth could have framed those words.

A dreadful smell suddenly filled the air, odious and caustic it was, like brine, but more acrid and sharp. I felt my lungs burn and my guts begin to churn. Then I heard an angry hissing sound and something solid but wet splashed against the inside of the window, making me jump from out of my skin.

I fled as far from the cabin as I could to the far end of the deck and remained there, huddled beneath a hanging charcoal brazier for warmth and comfort, shaking uncontrollably, until the light in Liestøl's cabin faded and a false dawn smeared the horizon with a grey, bleary glow.

\*\*\*

I was now convinced that we shared our vessel with some terrible demonic force. Had God abandoned us and left us for dead? Was the *Woolsey* was ferrying us straight to Hell? Liestøl seemed to hold the key to our fate, but who – or *what* – was it that he kept in his cabin away from prying eyes? I resolved to discover his secret, but decided I would need an ally, someone I could wholly trust.

I tried to confide in Billy Briggs, but he seemed lost inside himself somehow and had succumbed to a peculiar sense of self-pity. 'Sean, have you ever known love?' he asked me when at last we were able to speak in private, 'I mean, *truly* known love? A love that burns your heart until you feel it must surely burst? I thought I had, but I'm no longer sure...' And he took to wistful flights of fancy, recalling a girl in Bridport he'd once wooed, or a tailor's daughter from Dorchester.

I listened as best I could, but, in truth, I had no patience for his nonsense any more. For it seemed as if any common sense he had once possessed had abandoned him and he was trapped in a state of foolish childlike whimsy, unable to address the concerns of the present. I wondered if he had fallen victim to a malignant magical charm or if he'd always been so vain and immature, and my own self-preoccupation had stopped me from noticing.

The voyage had changed me in some way. For better or worse, I could not really say. I began to lament the loss of my wife, who I now saw as a source of stability and kindness, but I quickly brought myself up short, for I felt that I would slump into a dismal fugue like William Briggs. And so I steeled myself and sought help elsewhere.

I approached the taciturn Myers (for I felt there was something solid about the fellow that I could trust) and told him of my fears, thinking he might think me mad. As I spoke, he watched me closely with those small, piercing grey eyes of his. 'Ah,' he said, when I had finally finished my tale, 'so you've seen it too.'

He seemed hugely relieved, as if a great weight had been lifted from him. 'Liestøl is a decent enough man,' he explained, 'but has been cursed with a terrible burden. As I understand it, he first encountered this… this *creature* on an uncharted island in the Barents Sea. He sought to bottle it like an imp or genie, and to subjugate it to his will.'

I shuddered. "He told you all this?"

'In part, yes. He drinks sometimes to soothe his nerves and the whiskey is prone to loosen his tongue. He told me that he imprisoned the thing in a small iron box, as this metal can weaken and bind such creatures.'

'Is… is it a demon, then?' I asked him. 'A servant of Satan?'

'No. I believe it to be a sprite of some sort. An elemental force of nature that has dominion over water. A draugen, he calls it.' Myers rubbed at his eyes, as if suddenly weary. 'It made him a wealthy man, as he hoped it would, but there was an awful price to pay. He lost his wife and children to disease and fire. In the years that followed, his crew-mates and friends were taken from him, one at a time, and all in tragic circumstances. It would appear the sprite is malicious and has extracted a terrible payment for its imprisonment. And now Liestøl dares not form close associations with other human beings, for fear that they will become the draugen's next victim.'

I shook my head. The story was outlandish and fantastical, and yet, I myself had seen things in the last few days that made me inclined to believe him.

Myers continued: 'And so he has made a pact with this spiteful imp, agreeing to return it to its home, in return for lifting the curse.'

'I don't follow. Didn't you say he discovered it on the far side of the North Sea?'

'Aye, but the draugen's homeland is unanchored; it floats free on an unmapped, invisible sea, pulled here and there by tides that no mortal eye can see...' His voice trailed off, as if he could no longer bear to listen to his own words.

And then, from the rigging above came a sudden excited shout: 'Land Ahoy!'

***

By my reckoning, we should have been somewhere near the Azores, but for days both the water and the weather had seemed unfamiliar, as if we were in some other part of the globe entirely. Now, dead ahead of us lay an island – a stark outcrop of rock that appeared on no chart that I was familiar with and whose presence seemed to confirm Myers' tale.

We approached, flanked by rows of vicious, fang-shaped rocks that threatened to rip our hull like paper, so Liestøl took the wheel himself, guided by the strange, steam-driven mechanism, whose whining pitch would rise or fall, according to our proximity to the rocks. It was then that I came to realise that it was somehow sounding the depth of the water around us and had also guided us to this remote isle.

Above us loomed bleak crags splashed grey-white with guano. Eerie calls echoed down from gull colonies high on the cliffs overhead. Hughes, a sturdy, barrel-chested Welshman with a grey-streaked beard, had been studying them through his telescope, but now suddenly ran to the rails to be sick. Ashen-faced, he wiped a cord of spittle from his mouth. 'My God,' he said, and his voice trembled as a crew-mate offered him a nip from his flask. 'D-Did you see them? Their bodies were like owls, but their f-faces… I swear their faces were those of young children!'

Liestøl brought us in so close to the rocks that I felt catastrophe could only be moments away. Waves hammered against the grim, granite walls a few yards off the larboard bow, while the hideous calls of the hellbirds continued to drift down from above, adding to our unease. Nichols begged him to bring the vessel round, but Liestøl was like a man possessed now and would not be diverted from his course. Instead, he shouted for Myers to pay the crew an additional sovereign each upon land-fall, though this did little to improve our mood.

Beside us, the jagged rock-face folded in and out of itself like a morris-man's concertina and one of these crevices hid an enormous gash-like wound that was wide enough to accommodate the *Woolsey*.

We entered a vast cavern where the water was unnervingly calm and a gentle current slowly drew us deeper inside until the daylight faded completely and we were forced to light lanterns in order to fend off the dark. Hughes began to sing 'Abide With Me' in that rich baritone of his, others joining in until the captain hushed them down in order to hear the whine of his magical direction-engine.

Bats swooped down out of the void and flitted through the rigging: pale, bloodless albino things that emitted mournful cries. They circled us like awful little ghosts and I began to fear that we would become lost, left to drift forever in this sunless Afterlife.

We glided past huge stalagmites that might have been the marble columns of a temple once populated by Titans. And, in the knots and whorls of limestone, I fancied I saw the faces of forgotten kings and devils, created by the passage of our flickering lamps.

Ahead, we spotted a faint smudge of light that slowly grew larger until we could make out another, smaller island – an island within an island! *A sea within a sea!* – lit by a shaft of hazy sunlight that poured in through a hole in the cavern roof above.

***

Leaving a skeleton watch on board the *Woolsey*, we rowed ashore and landed on a beach of dark, volcanic ash and pumice-stone. Blind, eyeless fish swam in the swallows around our feet, their spiny bodies made from off-white bone. Nearby, we spied the beached and broken hulk of a galley from the age of Queen Elizabeth, its timbers now home to spindly, colourless things that resembled crayfish.

Liestøl had retreated into his own silent inner-world and appeared disinterested in issuing orders, so Myers recommended that we arm ourselves for the expedition inland. And so, we reluctantly trudged off the beach and up the embankment behind Myers and the Norwegian, bearing a hodgepodge of guns, swords, knives and clubs, with the brittle shells of trilobites crunching underfoot.

We set off into the undergrowth, hacking a path with our cutlasses and sabres, until Liestøl found a marker he'd scored in a tree some years earlier and pointed out to us a vague path through the foliage. In this dream-like, pale emerald limbo, the plants had grown queerly, their shoots and leaves sprouting directly upwards in search of this world's single source of light and warmth.

At the base of the trees the soil was rich, loamy and fragrant, home to twisted ochre toadstools and colonies of puffballs that exploded in our presence, sending up licorice-scented clouds of spores. Large black beetles and blood-red millipedes nipped at our ankles, while an unknown species of giant salamander watched us warily from within its imperious-looking collar-ruff.

A flight of bright orange dragonflies, their bodies as wide as a man's forearm, zigzagged past us on transparent, turquoise-veined wings. I turned to Briggsy, smiling for the first time in days at the sight of such wonders, but his features were rigid and cold, his thoughts lost in remembrance of some other time or place.

Late in the afternoon, we came upon a glade and found remains of what appeared to be an ancient graveyard. There were wooden crosses and rough headstones on which inscriptions had been scratched. One of my comrades, knowing I could read well, asked me what they said, but I replied that I could not read what seemed to me to be Latin. 'I can,' said Myers, somewhat sheepishly, and I swore that he blushed, 'I was schooled in a seminary.'

He crouched down and squinted at one of the grave markers, pulling its curtain of ivy to one side: 'See this? LVX… It means "Lux" or "Light." One of the signs of the Rosy Cross. A Rosicrucian is buried here: a soldier-mystic from one of the Hermetic Orders. The date reads 1723.'

Another cross he deciphered as being the resting-place of a Knight Templar: 'Stephen Morgyn, whose ship was lost in strange waters and here ran aground. Interred in 1284. May the Lord watch over him...'

'*Varikke*,' said Liestøl, as he stepped forward and finally spoke. 'It traps the unwary. It is like a lobster-pot; easy to enter, but impossible to escape. Unless you know how.' Tree-dappled sunlight streamed down on him from directly overhead, giving his sad, haunted features an odd, messianic quality. 'Over the years, dozens of poor wretches have been marooned here and left to the whims of Fate. I know, for I was one of them...' He shook his head, sadly.

'Varikke?' I asked.

'In English, you would call it: "was not"... Was-Not Island.' He smiled without humour or enthusiasm, as if at some private joke, clutched at a ball of frayed sacking in which I suspected was the iron box that Myers had mentioned. The rest of the crew were puzzled by his words and watched him intently, trying to follow his meaning. 'A myth, a place from out of folklore: an island that exists, yet, at the same time, does *not*. It is real, but it is not... solid...' He waved his hand in the air; vaguely, dismissively. 'It drifts from here to there like smoke or air... or a dream.'

'You are either mad, m'sieu, or a poet!' shouted Frenchie DuBois and he spat out a wad of well-chewed tobacco for punctuation. 'Pay us our dues now, so we can all go home.'

'That's enough!' said Myers, silencing the crew's ragged laughter before their mood turned to mutiny. A sense of unspoken unease had demoralised the ship for days. It had settled on the crew like a shroud and its presence would soon demand a scapegoat, an easy, tangible target such as Liestøl.

The Scandinavian held up the sacking and said: 'You have my word you will be paid in full. Just as soon as *this* is returned to its rightful – '

And then, in an instant, they were on us and Robert Simms went down screaming with one of the screeching horrors tearing at his throat with its awful teeth. The racket that these creatures made was truly horrible: they shrieked and hissed and drooled, rolling back their lips and gums to display rows of needle-sharp incisors.

It all happened so quickly that I could scarcely make out what they were as they erupted into the clearing. I pulled the French pistol from my waistband as one of the screeching abominations loped towards me: a baboon-like creature or a mandrill of some description with short, dark fur and bright, striped markings on its wide-nosed snout. But I was horrified to see that its eyes flashed with the cunning intelligence of a man.

The pistol used a percussion-cap, so was already charged and ready. Still, this screaming ape-thing had caught me off balance so my aim was poor, but the shot still caught it squarely on the shoulder and sent it spinning off sideways like a drunken dancer, leaving it disabled and howling in pain, not anger.

My shot was spent and I had no time to reload, so I grabbed the pistol's barrel, wielding its stout wooden handle like a club, and cracked it against the skull of another of the devil-monkeys, who was confounding one of my shipmates. The baboon-man was more surprised than hurt and turned to hiss at me maliciously, whereupon Declan made short work of it with the bayonet he'd inherited from his father, a soldier in the Royal Northumberland Fusiliers.

All around me, my shipmates desperately clubbed and hacked at the creatures in an attempt to fend them off. I looked around for Myers, who I spotted at the centre of a knot of men, rallying them. The canny fellow carefully raised his flintlock rifle and took aim at one of the creatures, whom he had correctly deduced to be the pack-leader: a bull-male who was larger and more vocal than the others and who was seemingly directing their attack with a series of frantic shrieks and high-pitched yelps. A puff of smoke came from behind the frizzen of his rifle, followed by a sharp crack that instantly felled the baboon. On the ground it shuddered and shook and howled in pain until the pack retreated, dragging the old bull back into the tree line.

The last few minutes had left me breathless and shaking, so I sat and rested against a headstone for a moment. As I reloaded I was joined by Briggsy, whose face was scratched and bloody, though his wounds were superficial and would quickly heal.

'Who will love me now?' He pawed at his face and wailed like a lost soul. A frightened, lonely child. Tears ran down his cheeks and mingled freely with his blood.

\*\*\*

At the island's epicentre we came upon a body of water, a small, unnaturally circular lake set in a clearing free of trees. A strange foreboding atmosphere hung over the place: there was no birdsong nor insect chatter, no ripples flittered across its surface; instead, an odd, oppressive silence hung in the air and the light that filtered down from above endued the water with an eerie glow.

   Liestøl stopped us when we tried to give refreshment to comrades that had been mauled by the ape-men, saying that a terrible evil lurked within the water and it would do them great harm if they were to drink from it. I could see that the crew were extremely agitated and vexed by Liestøl's eccentric ways. He had hurried us on from the graveyard, explaining that any further delays would endanger us. 'I already have too much blood on my hands,' he had moaned. 'I can bear no more.'

Now he approached the edge of the pool and unwrapped a metal box from the cloth he carried. He pressed a series of tiny brass studs on its side in a certain sequence and spoke some words under his breath in a guttural language that did not sound like his own.

Crouching down stiffly by the side of the lake, he opened the lid of the box whereupon a spiral of water shot out from within and twisted rapidly through the air like a tiny waterspout. I confess I gasped in amazement along with my ship-mates. Some of them began to mutter and cross themselves, backing away from the Norwegian and this queer phenomenon.

The twisting column of liquid arced through the air and down into the pool as if it were alive, draining itself into the larger body of water. I then noticed the same queer smell I had encountered that fearful night on board the *Woolsey*. Lights sprang from the box and seemed to bob up and down in the air, dancing like fireflies around the spinning jet of water.

More and more water issued forth from the box – far more than could have possibly been held within – so much so that I began to doubt my own sanity, until finally it stopped.

Liestøl shouted out across the water, in English (for our benefit, I presume): 'Hear me, Draugen! I have honoured our pact and have returned you to your birthplace as I said I would. Now begone and plague me no further!' He turned to face us with sad eyes and a weary expression as if asking for our forgiveness, saying: 'Finally. It is over. We can all return home now.'

But it was not to be. Something was rising to the surface, silently, from the centre of the lake and we all watched in mute astonishment.

There were four of them: nymphs or naiads or some other exotic creature of the sea, I suppose. Their beauty was without peer. They had skin that glistened and shone, catching the light subtly like mother-of-pearl. Their hair was long and flowed free, woven from deep, dark turquoise and aquamarine; it seemed alive, to ripple and flow like swirling tidal eddies in a wave-swept cove. Their laughter was rich and musical as they frolicked and bathed one another with water from large, multi-coloured conch-shells. I am not ashamed to confess that, like my ship-mates, I was irresistibly drawn to them, hypnotised, like a moth by a flickering flame.

Unable to resist their unearthly beauty, we stumbled forward as if drunk, wading out into the water to greet them. My conscious mind sensed there was something unnatural about these women – something unfathomably *wrong* – but I was spellbound, a victim of my own lustful impulses and could do little more than follow my companions.

Being something of a ladies man, Billy seemed more afflicted worse than most. His jaw was clenched in a tight, lecherous grin and he pulled at his shirt, trying to remove it as he ran towards these giggling nymphs who made no pretence at modesty. Being a dreamy sort with a hedonistic temperament, I wondered if he somehow felt their magical pull more keenly than the rest of us, and this is what had recently made him sullen and dissatisfied.

I tried to avert my eyes in the hope it would break the spell, concentrating instead on my own distorted reflection in the water below. This seemed to help somewhat and, slowly, I began to realise that the women and the pool were just an elaborate illusion: a few yards ahead of us, the water darkened as the rocky shelf dropped away down into a bottomless abyss. I understood now that these creatures were trying to lure us out beyond the edge of this precipice.

As we neared the chasm I saw glimpses of awful, unnatural shapes lurking far below. What appeared to be a pond or small lake was, in fact, merely the surface of an immense vertical ocean that stretched downwards into dark, fathomless depths.

I tried to give voice to my fears but my mouth was numb and paralysed, my jaw trapped in a dull rictus of stupefaction, and I could do little more than march forward toward my doom.

Then I heard a shout from behind me. It was Liestøl yelling a desperate warning. 'Nooo!' he cried with a desperate sob. 'Beware! They are not what they seem!'

And he splashed his way out towards us, seemingly immune to their siren-like charms. *Draugvetter! Draugvetter!* he cried. 'Turn back! These things will drag you down to Hell! They are draugenspawn! Daughters of the Draugen!'

His words helped break the spell and I saw one or two of my comrades hesitate and look around as if waking from a slumber. But Billy had already almost reached them and he launched himself, shirtless and laughing, at one of the glistening dream-nymphs. He took her into his arms and kissed her. She giggled and smiled and whispered something into his ear, pulling away coyly and attempting to lure him the last few feet out into the deeper water.

But Liestøl ran at them both, shouting

hysterically, while the rest of the crew looked on in confusion.

'No!' he screamed, 'Get away from her or she will kill you! Too many have already died because of me!'

Billy recoiled – and just in time! The nymph's features twisted and melted like candle wax, softening and then suddenly flowing freely like water to reveal something black, vile and ancient underneath. The air filled with a terrible stench, of brine mixed with burning human hair or hot pitch. Billy screamed, seemingly paralysed by its transformation, but Liestøl, yelling in Norwegian, pushed him backwards, away from harm.

The four nymphs now stood revealed as little more than constructs, artificial fabrications whose features were formed from some variety of magical water. The liquid shifted and flowed, boiled away like steam from their true features, leaving four ghastly hissing things, their flesh dry and brittle and blackened by age, that resembled lightning-blasted tree-trunks.

Their bodies stretched and lengthened obscenely, oozing slime and pale, watery mucous as they writhed and coiled in and out of each other with an unearthly serpentine grace.

They closed around Liestøl like the four fingers of some enormous hand. He swore and cursed at them in his native tongue, until I heard his ribs snap and the air was squeezed from his lungs. They held him in their grip, shaking him like a grotesque broken puppet, before dragging him down beneath the surface of the water, leaving only a faint trail of bubbles in their wake.

As we ran for the safety of dry land, the water heaved and boiled behind us, as if a behemoth was rising up from the murky depths below. A tangled mass of tentacles suddenly erupted: dark, knotted and rotten-looking, they were – the colour of old driftwood – yet somehow also sinuous, like the arms of an octopus, as they slapped at the water and probed blindly for fresh victims.

Then a grotesque gelatinous form followed them up out of the water and extended an array of eyes on fleshy slug-like stalks. This... *thing* was partially transparent, boneless and translucent like a jellyfish with crests and elaborate fan-shaped frills. I could make out structures embedded deep within it: pink-tinged tubes, organs bloated with purple-blue blood which pulsed and quivered with unnatural life. I looked on in horror as Hughes and young Tommy Quinn were snatched up by its appendages and dragged backwards through the water, screaming for mercy, towards a soft, blubbery maw.

Then from the monster came the dreadful, parrot-like squawking that I recognised from Liestøl's cabin and I knew then that the draugen was no mere imp or sprite, but the fearsome, undisputed king of some bottomless ocean that existed far beneath this island. Somehow I sensed that, like an iceberg, this was just a small part of the entity's enormous mass and that its bulk extended downwards for miles, lord of all it surveyed.

*Had Liestøl merely captured some minute part of this creature?* I wondered. And then on the ground beside me I spotted the iron box that he had discarded and an idea – a peculiar intuition – came uninvited into my mind.

I snatched up the box. It was engraved with arcane sigils and writings, and – remembering that the creature had an aversion to iron – I hurled it as hard as I could at the creature's repulsive bulk. As the box made contact with the draugen there was a sudden and unexpected explosive concussion, as if I had thrown a short-fused bomb.

The transparent, jellied skin ruptured violently, spilling out part of its contents, as if it had been gutted with a knife. Steam and acrid smoke poured from the wound as the creature squirmed and thrashed around in the water, soaking us with its spray and inadvertently releasing its victims.

The iron box had burned a hole into its body and now continued to scald its innards from within. The injured draugen squawked like an angry parrot, unable to eject the object that was causing it such discomfort.

We ran for the relative safety of the woods, dragging our wounded along as best we could. Behind us, the creature lashed out, its limbs cutting through the air like thick ropes – barbed gelatine whips that lashed at the undergrowth in impotent rage. In time, its howls of indignation faded into the distance and were replaced by the sounds of our own breathless flight.

***

I remember little of our escape from that terrible place, though I now seem to recall that we later paused to tend to the sick and injured. Mindful of the savage baboon-men that haunted the graveyard, we quickly buried our dead there next to the Templars and the other lost souls who had been victims of Varikke Island.

A prayer was said for the tragic Liestøl, who I now accepted as a decent, if misguided man. Any sins originally committed in the name of greed had been redeemed, in my eyes at least, by his final selfless act of bravery.

\*\*\*

Our voyage home, with Myers in command, was uneventful and felt more like a slow awakening from some terrible dream. Myers paid each member of the crew an equal share, as had been promised, including the widows of those who had been lost. He retained mastery of the *Woolsey* and offered me a place as first mate, but I declined and instead apprenticed with Martin Turner, the shipwright, where I learned carpentry and acquired skills sufficient enough for me to set up a business using my share of Liestøl's money.

My wife, seeing I had resolved to change my ways, soon had me back in her bed and I knew from that moment on that we would grow grey and fade into dust together, and this no longer frightened nor disturbed me.

As for Billy Briggs, well, he had also changed – and not for the better. Sometimes, I would encounter him on the quayside, alone and taciturn, staring forlornly out to sea. Seemingly at odds with the world and all within it, he slowly drank himself into dissolution.

In time, I prospered in my own way and began to grow as a man, so that I now look back at my younger self with a certain degree of bemusement. As I write these words, I can hear the laughter of my grandchildren as they play in the courtyard outside. Looking back on the strange events of that tragic yet oddly life-affirming voyage, there is no sound in this world – or the next – that I would rather hear.

Printed in Great Britain
by Amazon